FIONA FRENCH won the 1986 Kate Greenaway Medal
for her book *Snow White in New York*. In 1992 *Anancy and Mr Dry-Bone*,
her first book for Frances Lincoln, was selected for Children's Books
of the Year and won the Sheffield Book Award. It was followed by
Jill Paton Walsh's *Pepi and the Secret Names* chosen as one of
Child Education's Best Story Books of 1994, *Jamil's Clever Cat,*
Joyce Dunbar's *The Glass Garden* and *The Smallest Samurai.*
Her latest books are the stained-glass Bible stories
Bethlehem, Easter and *Paradise.*

For Tim and Nathalie Bacon

The coastal and interior regions of what is now California were once inhabited by seven distinct groupings of Miwok Indians. This tale is one of the surviving vestiges of an elaborate culture of hunter-gatherers which has virtually vanished. There remain only about 200 Miwok, equally divided between the interior and the coast. For this retelling, the author has drawn on the following sources: *The Folk-Lore Record, Volume V* (London, 1882) and *The Voice of Coyote,* J. Frank Dobie (Little, Brown & Co., Boston, 1949).

Lord of the Animals copyright © Frances Lincoln Limited 1997
Text and illustrations copyright © Fiona French 1997

First published in Great Britain in 1997 by
Frances Lincoln Children's Books, 4 Torriano Mews,
Torriano Avenue, London NW5 2RZ
www.franceslincoln.com

This edition published in Great Britain in 2008 and in the USA in 2009

British Library Cataloguing in Publication Data available on request

ISBN 978-1-84507-916-1

Printed in China

9 8 7 6 5 4 3 2 1

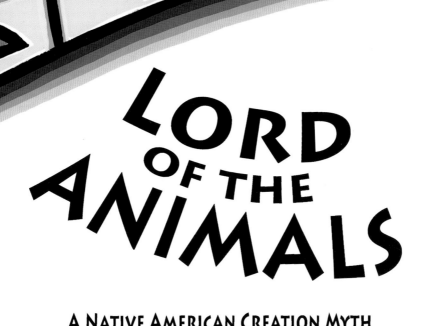

LORD
OF THE
ANIMALS

A NATIVE AMERICAN CREATION MYTH

FIONA FRENCH

F

FRANCES LINCOLN
CHILDREN'S BOOKS

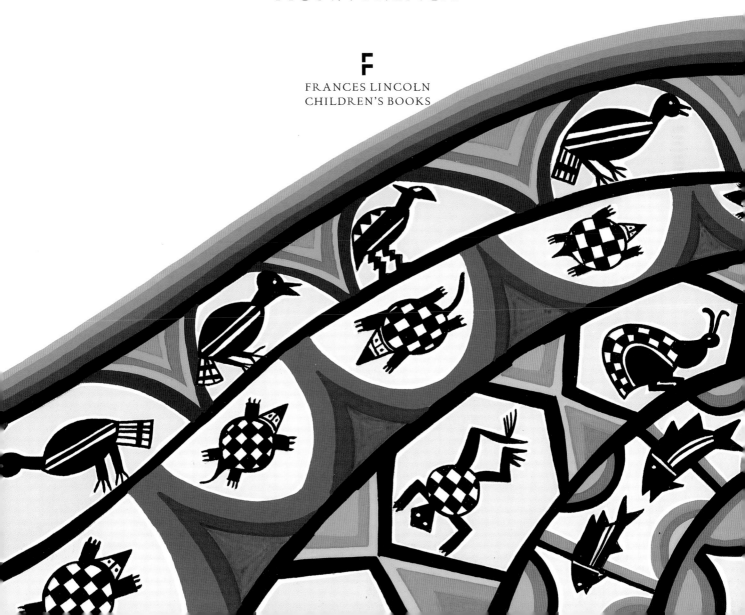

Long ago, Coyote created the world and all the creatures in it. Then he sat on the river bank and gathered a council of animals around him.

"We must decide how to make the Lord of the Animals," he said. "If he is to rule over us, he has to be a very superior creature."

"I agrrree," purred the mountain lion. "The Lord of the Animals must be strong, and he must be swift and silent."

"No, no," said the
grizzly bear. "He must
have a big growl."

"The Lord of the Animals
must have antlers," said the deer.
"His eyes must see everything and his
ears must hear the lightest
footstep in the grass."

"But antlers would get caught in the trees," said the sheep. "The Lord of the Animals must have horns rolled tightly on each side of his head so that he can butt hard."

"How stupid you all are," said Coyote. "You want to make our ruler just like yourselves. You might as well take one of your own cubs and call it the Lord of the Animals.

The Lord of the Animals
should be better than any of us.
His voice should be even more tuneful
than mine. He should run fast and
silently after his prey.

"His feet must be like a bear's, so that he can
stand upright. And the deer is right: his eyes must
be sharp and his ears must hear the smallest sound
so that he can be ready for danger. I don't think
he needs a tail. It is a house for fleas.

"And," Coyote said,
  "his skin should be smoother
   than a fish's scales."
The beaver protested,
  "But without a tail, how will he
   guide himself under water?"

The eagle said, "The Lord of the Animals must have wings to fly above us all."

"And he must burrow deep in the earth," said the mole.

"He must see in the dark," said the owl.

"And what about some nice long whiskers too?" said the smallest mouse.

"How silly!"
"How stupid!"
Fur and feathers
began to fly.

The owl flew at the beaver,
the mouse bit the lion and
the bear sat on the mole.

"Stop!" cried Coyote.
"Let us each take
a lump of river mud
and make a model of
the Lord of the Animals.
Then we will choose
the best one."

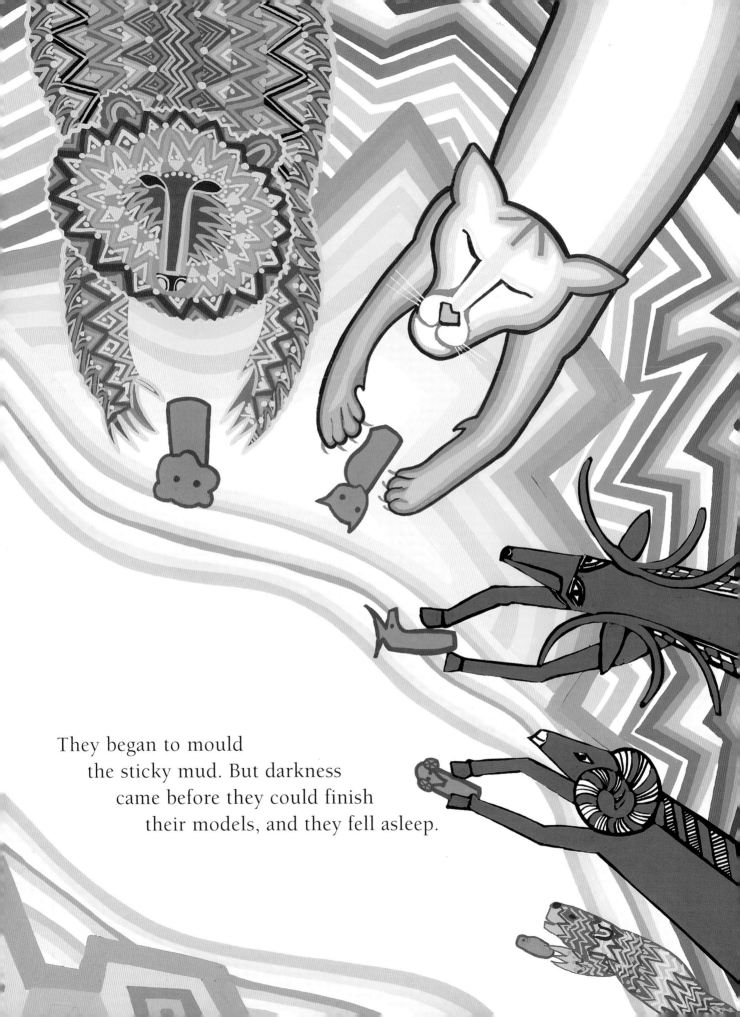

They began to mould
the sticky mud. But darkness
came before they could finish
their models, and they fell asleep.

But crafty Coyote stayed awake all night and made his model by the light of the moon. The river lapped gently over the other models and they disappeared into the water.

In the morning, before the other animals were awake, Coyote finished his model and gave him life.

That is why his eyes can see into the distance and his ears can hear the slightest sound.

Like a bear, he can stand on two legs, and his voice is tuneful.

His skin is smooth and he can swim like a fish in the sea.

But above all, he is Lord of the Animals because he is cunning and clever - just like Coyote!

MORE TITLES BY FIONA FRENCH
FROM FRANCES LINCOLN CHILDREN'S BOOKS

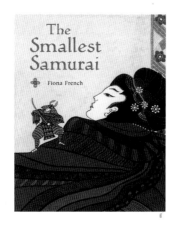

The Smallest Samurai

Little Inchkin is only as big as a lotus flower,
but he has the courage of a Samurai warrior.
How he proves his valour, wins the hand of a
princess, and is granted his dearest wish by the
Lord Buddha is charmingly retold in this
Tom Thumb legend of old Japan.

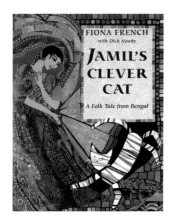

Jamil's Clever Cat
A Folk Tale from Bengal

Sardul is the cleverest of cats. When he learns that
his master, Jamil the weaver, dreams of marrying a
princess, he resolves to make Jamil's wish come true.
But how can he make Jamil appear the richest man
in the world, and so win the princess's hand?

Anancy and Mr Dry-Bone
Poor Anancy and rich Mr Dry-Bone both want to
marry Miss Louise, but *she* wants to marry the man
who can make her laugh. She does not laugh at
Mr Dry-Bone's conjuring tricks and acrobatics so
Anancy decides to ask the animals for help in
winning her over. A delightful story, based on
characters from traditional Caribbean and West
African folk-tales, with vibrant illustrations.

Frances Lincoln titles are available from all good bookshops.
You can also buy books and find out more about your favourite titles,
authors and illustrators on our website: www.franceslincoln.com